Pebble® Plus

Let's Look at Light

Is It Light, or Dark?

by Mari Schuh

PEBBLE
a capstone imprint

Pebble Plus is published by Pebble
1710 Roe Crest Drive, North Mankato, Minnesota 56003
www.mycapstone.com

Library of Congress Cataloging-in-Publication Data
Names: Schuh, Mari C., 1975- author.
Title: Is it light or dark? / by Mari Schuh.
Description: North Mankato, Minnesota : Pebble, a Capstone imprint, [2020] |
  Series: Pebble plus. Let's look at light | Audience: Ages 4-8. | Audience:
  K to grade 3. | Includes bibliographical references and index.
Identifiers: LCCN 2018060249| ISBN 9781977108937 (hardcover) | ISBN
  9781977110404 (pbk.) | ISBN 9781977108975 (ebook pdf)
Subjects: LCSH: Light--Juvenile literature. | Light--Properties--Juvenile
  literature.
Classification: LCC QC360 .S3825 2020 | DDC 535--dc23
LC record available at https://lccn.loc.gov/2018060249

Editorial Credits
Karen Aleo, editor; Kyle Grenz, designer; Tracy Cummins, media researcher; Laura Manthe, production specialist

Photo Credits
iStockphoto: Jonas Velin, 19, skynesher, 5, woolzian, 21; Shutterstock: all_about_people, 9, Guenter Albers, 17, Kevin Cass, Cover Bottom, Lillac, Cover Back, liseykina, 7, Mike Pellinni, Cover Top, Motortion Films, 15, sema srinouljan, 13, upslim, 11, Xseon, 1

Note to Parents and Teachers

The Let's Look at Light set supports national standards related to light and energy. This book describes and illustrates lightness and darkness. The images support early readers in understanding the text. The repetition of words and phrases helps early readers learn new words. This book also introduces early readers to subject-specific vocabulary words, which are defined in the Glossary section. Early readers may need assistance to read some words and to use the Table of Contents, Glossary, Read More, Internet Sites, Critical Thinking, and Index sections of the book.

All internet sites appearing in back matter were available and accurate when this book was sent to press.

Printed in China.
1654

Table of Contents

A Sunny Day

Today is a sunny day!

The sun shines brightly.

Sunlight is a kind of light.

All About Light

Sunlight and other kinds

of light help us see.

Sunlight comes from

nature. People make some

lights like light bulbs.

Light moves quickly from

one place to another.

It bounces off objects.

Then it travels to our eyes.

That's how we see objects.

Light and Dark

Light helps us see the world around us.

Bright lights make things easy to see.

Lamps help us read.

Turn off the lights!

Now it is dark.

There is not a lot of light.

It's hard to see anything.

13

Objects can block light.
Kids make forts with
blankets. Blankets block
the light in the room.
Inside the fort is dark.

Day and Night

The sun shines during

the day.

It is light outside.

It's easy to see trees,

roads, and animals.

At night, it is dark outside.
Part of Earth is turned
away from the sun.
There is no sunlight.

We need lights to help us see at night. People use candles, nightlights, and flashlights. Light helps us in so many ways!

Glossary

flashlight—a small light that people carry that uses a battery

nature—everything in the world that isn't made by people

nightlight—a small light that plugs into an outlet so people can see at night

sunlight—light that comes from the sun

Read More

Dunne, Abbie. *Light.* Physical Science. North Mankato, Minn.: Capstone Press, 2017.

Rivera, Andrea. *Light.* Zoom in on Science Concepts. Minneapolis: Abdo Zoom, 2017.

Spilsbury, Louise and Richard. *Light and Dark.* Exploring Light. Chicago: Heinemann Raintree, 2016.

Internet Sites

Easy Science for Kids: All About Light and Dark
https://easyscienceforkids.com/all-about-light-and-dark/

BBC: Light and Dark Worksheet
http://downloads.bbc.co.uk/schools/teachers/ks2worksheets/
bbc_teachers_ks2_science_worksheet_light_and_dark.pdf

Super-cool stuff!

Check out projects, games, and lots more at
www.capstonekids.com

Critical Thinking Questions

1. Describe how light travels.
2. Name three kinds of light.
3. Why is it dark at night?

Index